'Brother!' shouted Noah . . . 'I'm going to build a boat. A big one. 300 cubits long, 50 wide, 30 high. Three decks. Out of gopher wood.'

'That will need an awful lot of trees, Noah. Who's going to cut them all down?'

'You are,' said Noah.

You've probably heard the story of Noah's Ark, but did you know it was really Noah's brother Hazardikla-doram – Yessah for short – who played the most important part in the building and the voyage of the Ark?

Although Yessah was older than Noah, he was a small, bald, timid old man, and it was huge, bearded, bossy Noah who gave the orders. But Yessah was a patient old fellow, and his hard work and love of animals (he was a vegetarian, of course) ensured that Noah's great plan got off the ground!

Another witty and affectionate tale from one of Puffin's most popular authors.

Dick King-Smith was a farmer in Gloucestershire for many years before deciding to become a primary school teacher, but he now writes full-time. He has more recently become well known for his television appearances. He was winner of the Guardian Children's Fiction Award for his novel *The Sheep-Pig*.

Other books by Dick King-Smith

Dick King-Smith

Noah's Brother

Illustrated by Ian Newsham

PUFFIN BOOKS

PUFFIN BOOKS

Published by the Penguin Group
27 Wrights Lane, London W8 5TZ, England
Viking Penguin Inc., 40 West 23rd Street, New York, New York 10010, USA
Penguin Books Australia Ltd, Ringwood, Victoria, Australia
Penguin Books Canada Ltd, 2801 John Street, Markham, Ontario, Canada L3R 1B4
Penguin Books (NZ) Ltd, 182–190 Wairau Road, Auckland 10, New Zealand

Penguin Books Ltd, Registered Offices: Harmondsworth, Middlesex, England

First published by Victor Gollancz Ltd 1986
Published in Puffin Books 1988
3 5 7 9 10 8 6 4

Printed in England by Clays Ltd, St Ives plc
Filmset in Monophoto Sabon

Chapter One

'Brother!' shouted Noah in his great booming voice.

'Yessah?'

'I'm going to build a boat. A big one. 300 cubits long, 50 wide, 30 high. Three decks. Out of gopher wood.'

'That will need an awful lot of trees, Noah. Who's going to cut them all down?'

'You are,' said Noah.

It is an interesting fact (which few people know) that Noah had an older brother. Quite a bit older, actually, since Noah was 600 years old and his brother 708.

Everybody knows who eventually sailed in the Ark: there was Noah and Mrs Noah, their three sons Shem, Ham and Japheth, and Mrs Shem, Mrs Ham and Mrs Japheth; and, of course, two of every animal on earth. But down below, in the lowest, darkest part of the belly of the Ark, was someone else: Noah's brother.

Hazardikladoram was Noah's brother's real name, but nobody in the family ever called him that; it was much too much of a mouthful and besides, everyone had a particular way of addressing him. Noah always called him 'Brother', Mrs Noah only ever said 'Hey, you', and as for Shem, Ham and Japheth, they had invented a nickname for their uncle while they were still quite small.

They soon noticed that whenever their father (who was a huge, bearded, bossy old man) spoke to his brother (who was a small, bald, timid old man), it was to give him some kind of order.

'Do this! Do that!' said Noah to his brother, and always Hazardikladoram meekly answered, 'Yessah!' So the boys took to calling him 'Uncle Yessah', and later, when they were grown up and married, just plain 'Yessah'.

Yessah felt pretty fed up, the morning that Noah told him to start cutting down gopher trees. It

wasn't the work he minded – he was pretty fit for his age – it was the way the family treated him. He grumbled to himself in between swings of his axe:

'I shouldn't mind a "Please" (thunk), or a "Thank you" (thunk) and a bit of respect (thunk). After all, I am the oldest (thunk) member of the family,' and on the word 'family' he gave the gopher tree a specially hard wallop and it fell down.

As it fell, two white doves fluttered out of its branches.

'Oh sorry!' gasped Yessah, who was very fond of animals and had a special way with them, 'didn't know you were up there, my dears.'

The doves flew down and perched, one on each of Yessah's thin shoulders.

'Peace,' said one softly in his left ear; 'Goodwill,' said the other in his right; and then they flew gently away, wing-tip to wing-tip, cooing sweet nothings to one another.

Yessah suddenly felt much happier, and began

chopping down gopher trees right, left and centre. How I do like animals, he thought as he worked; and it was just as well he did, for in a few weeks Noah gave him another order.

By that time the Ark was pretty well finished. To be fair, the rest of the family had worked hard too: while the women busily prepared great stores of food, Noah and his three sons collected all the trees that Yessah had felled, and sawed them into planks. They had a lot of fun building the boat, though there was one job they did not fancy, which was covering every bit of the boat with pitch to make it watertight. The pitch was horribly black, thick and sticky, so they gave the job to Yessah.

Then one morning, when everything was ship-shape at last, Noah stood on the poop-deck of the Ark and shouted, 'Brother!'

'Yessah?' said Yessah, hurrying aft.

'Listen carefully, Brother,' said Noah. 'I want two of every kind of animal on the earth. Every beast, every bird, every creeping thing. Two of each. One male, one female. Get it?'

'Yessah. But who's going to collect all that lot?'

'You are,' said Noah.

Chapter Two

'But why do you want them all?'

'That,' said Noah, 'is my business, Brother. You just round 'em up.'

Yessah went off, shaking his head. 'First he builds a whopping great boat miles from the sea, and then he wants to collect two of every kind of animal. Whatever for?'

Yessah hurried back to Noah.

'You're not going to eat these animals, Noah, are you?' he said.

It is an interesting fact (which few people know) that Noah's brother was a vegetarian. All the rest of the family gorged themselves daily on the meat of ox and sheep and goat, but Yessah had never harmed any animal, much less killed one in order to swallow its flesh.

Now, though the crown of his head was only as

high as the tip of Noah's beard, he faced up to his younger brother bravely.

'Because if you are, you can count me out.'

'Brother,' said Noah in quite a quiet voice, 'I give you my word that not one of the animals going into the Ark will be killed. Anyway, Mrs Noah's got a galley full of fresh meat.'

Yessah shuddered, but Noah did not notice because he was staring at the sky. For months it had been blue and clear, but now suddenly, as Yessah saw when he followed his brother's gaze, there were one or two clouds about; they were rather sulky-looking little black clouds.

'D'you think the weather's going to break?' he said.

Noah looked down at him and frowned. His voice suddenly grew much louder.

'I don't think,' he said, 'I know! And if you don't get a move on, and start collecting those animals, something else is going to break – your neck! GET ON WITH IT!'

'Yessah!' said Noah's brother.

*

At first he found the job fairly easy. He began by catching animals that couldn't argue about being caught; and soon there were pairs of creatures like worms and snails and beetles and frogs wriggling, crawling, scurrying and hopping up the gangway into the Ark.

Shem, Ham and Japheth took turns to stand on guard and make sure these early arrivals did not turn round and wriggle, crawl, scurry or hop straight off again.

But when Yessah began tackling some of the larger animals, he met with opposition. Not surprisingly, none of them wanted to volunteer.

Stubborn ones like donkeys refused to listen to him, bad-tempered ones like camels told him to get lost, and intelligent ones like the great apes wanted to know why.

'Give us a good reason, Yessah,' said a big silverbacked gorilla, 'for agreeing to be shut up in a stuffy old boat. We're perfectly happy as we are. Why do you need us?'

'I don't know,' said Yessah uncomfortably, 'only Noah knows.'

'Oh, Noah!' said the gorilla in a rather scornful voice, and he walked away, chewing a bamboo shoot.

'What am I going to do?' said Yessah to the two white doves, Peace and Goodwill, who now went everywhere with him, perched on his thin shoulders. 'How can I persuade the animals to come into the Ark if I don't know why Noah wants them? There must be a reason but he won't tell me.'

'Leave it to us, Master,' said Peace.

'We'll ask around, Master,' said Goodwill.

'We'll ask all the other birds,' they said.

They began by asking the owl, believing him to be wise.

'Why d'you think Noah's doing this?' they said.

'Who,' said the owl.

'Noah.'

'Who who,' said the owl.

Peace and Goodwill looked at each other and shook their heads.

They asked the guinea-fowl, but he only said, 'Go back! Go back!' They asked the bunting, but he only said, 'A little bit of bread and no cheese!' And they asked the song-thrush, but he only said, 'Did he do it? Did he do it? Come out! Come out!'

They asked the kittiwake who said, 'Kittiwake!' and the peewit who said, 'Peewit!' When they asked the kookaburra, he burst into fits of laughter, and

the ostrich said nothing because his head was buried in the sand.

At last, very tired, Peace and Goodwill came across a yellow-billed cuckoo.

It is an interesting fact (which few people know) that the yellow-billed cuckoo's other name is the rain-bird, because when he's noisy it means there's going to be a downpour; and this one was making a tremendous racket.

The doves listened carefully to what he was saying, and then flew back to Yessah, who was gingerly shoving a couple of hedgehogs up the gangway.

'Master! Master!' they cried. 'We've found the reason! We know what the Ark is for. It's going to rain and rain and rain, for forty days and forty nights, and the whole earth will be flooded!'

'Who told you?'

'The rain-bird, Master,' said the white doves.

Yessah had been so busy trying to round up animals, he hadn't had time to think about the weather. Now he looked up at the sky and saw that it was filled with clouds, huge angry clouds. At the same moment a huge angry face appeared high above him on the Ark.

'Get on with it, Brother!' yelled Noah. 'We haven't got a quarter of the animals yet!'

Wearily, Yessah set off again. His heart was heavy. If the rain-bird was right, and he did not doubt this, all the beautiful animals on the earth would be drowned, except for two of each sort. He understood Noah's plan now. But how was he to choose which pair, of hippos or kangaroos or antelope? Once they all knew of the terrible danger that threatened them, there would be a fearful stampede as they all rushed for the safety of the Ark.

'It's awful,' he said, 'but only two of each kind can be told, secretly. Somehow I must choose a pair of each, one male, one female, and whisper the news of the coming Flood in their ears.' He looked again at the darkening sky. 'But how can I possibly do this in time?'

'You can't,' said Peace.

'But we can,' said Goodwill.

'How?'

'Simple,' they said. 'We'll ask help from all the birds who don't care tuppence about a flood – the ducks and the geese and the swans, the seagulls and the cormorants and the albatrosses. None of them need to come into the Ark.'

'We'll divide the job up amongst them,' said Peace, 'so that one pair of every kind of animal is told.'

'Except the fish,' Goodwill added, and off they flew.

Before long Noah and his family began to see pairs of animals on the move everywhere. Two by two they came: down from the mountains or out of the forests or across the plains, and they all went into the Ark. Up the gangway they went; lions and tigers, wolves and bears, elephants and giraffes,

one male and one female of every kind. Yessah
stood at the foot of the gangway, ticking off their
names on a long list that he had made.

Last but one a pair of tortoises lumbered slowly
up, just ahead of a couple of hares who had stopped
for a nap on the way.

Out of the gathering gloom two white shapes
dropped down and settled on their master's thin
shoulders.

Yessah shouted up to his brother standing on the poop-deck high above.

'That's it, Noah,' he called, 'that's the lot,' and even as he spoke a big drop of water plopped down on his bald head, and then another. Suddenly the storm broke and the rain came down in torrents.

Above the noise of the wind and the downpour came the sound of Noah's great voice.

'Pull up the gangway!' he shouted, and Shem, Ham and Japheth pulled it up.

'Hey!' cried Noah's brother as the storm roared. 'Hey! Hang on a minute! What about me?'

But nobody seemed to hear.

Chapter Three

Within a few moments Yessah looked like a drowned rat; within an hour he would certainly have looked like a drowned man, so quickly did the Flood rise, if Peace and Goodwill had not flown into the Ark for help. Even so, it was a very close thing.

Once the gangway had been raised there was no way for Yessah to get aboard. Even the port-holes of the lowest deck were far above his head. The water rose to his waist, to his chest, to his chin, until at last he stood on tiptoe, his head thrown back. As he gulped what he felt to be his final breath, he saw the doves peering out.

'Rescue's on the way, Master!' they called. 'Start swimming!'

'I can't swim!' they heard him cry, and then the swirling waters closed over his bald crown.

They say when people are drowning, the whole of their past lives flash through their minds. Yessah's whirling thoughts had got as far as the birth of his baby brother, Noah (when he himself had been a youngster of 108), and then suddenly something very thick and very strong curled itself around his body, and plucked him from the depths.

When Yessah came to, he was lying flat on the planking of the Ark's lowest deck. A ring of assorted faces peered down at him, including two worried little white ones.

'Master!' cried Peace and Goodwill. 'Are you all right?'

'What . . . how . . . who . . .?' spluttered Yessah.

'It was one of the pythons,' said Peace. 'It swam out and coiled itself round you, and hoisted you aboard.'

'And then,' said Goodwill, 'one of the elephants sucked most of the water out of you with its trunk, and one of the gorillas thumped your chest to get your heart beating again.'

Yessah struggled into a sitting position. He

felt sore inside and out but very glad to be alive.

'Oh, thank you all,' he said, 'especially the python. Where are you, my dear?'

'Here,' said a voice, and a great flat blunt-snouted face pushed itself forward.

'You saved my life!' exclaimed Yessah.

'Makes a change,' said the python. 'One of my ancestors spoiled the life of one of yours.'

'Who was he?'

'Chap called Adam,' said the serpent.

At that instant they all felt the deck move beneath them. The Ark was afloat.

High above on the poop-deck, Noah and his three sons felt the movement and peered overside through the rain-filled darkness. They had loaded the Ark carefully, putting all the heavy beasts like elephants, hippos and rhinos on to the lowest deck, and the boat seemed to be riding steadily.

'Get hold of your uncle,' said Noah, 'and tell him to go below to make sure everything's water-tight.' He strode off.

Shem, Ham and Japheth looked at each other.

'Oh Lord!' said Shem.

'Clean forgot about the old geezer,' said Ham.

'He'll be food for the fishes by now,' said Japheth.

'Father will be livid!' they said.

At that moment Noah's brother staggered out of one of the hatchways. Shem, Ham and Japheth heaved a great sigh of relief, not because their uncle's life had been spared, but because they had been spared their father's wrath. They turned upon Hazardikladoram as one man.

'Get below!' bawled Shem. 'Make sure there are no leaks!'

'And while you're about it,' shouted Ham, 'you can feed the animals!'

'You can muck 'em out too!' bellowed Japheth.

Wearily, Yessah went below again. All night, while the family slept, he worked at the tasks his nephews had set him. By the time he had finished he was aching all over, filthy dirty and very hungry.

It was broad daylight again when at last he made his way to the galley. Perhaps, he thought, there'll

be a nice hot bowl of vegetable soup for me. I'm starving.

But when he got there, Mrs Noah came out.

'Hey you!' she said, 'take this,' and she thrust a big plate of roast beef at him.

'It's meat,' said Yessah. 'I can't eat that.'

Mrs Noah looked at him disgustedly.

'I should jolly well think you can't,' she said. 'It's for Noah. Hurry up and take it to him, he's had a long, hard night.'

'Dirty, lazy old thing,' she said to her three daughters-in-law when Yessah had gone, 'he's no better than an animal. Why he had to be saved from the Flood, God alone knows.'

Chapter Four

In truth, if Yessah was no better than the animals, he could have been proud of the fact; for they could not have been more kindly and thoughtful.

Once they realized what a state the old man was in, they all wanted to help. Noah and the rest, they knew, killed animals for food, but Noah's brother had never hurt a flea. They got together to see what they could do.

The first thing Yessah needed, they decided, was food. This turned out to be an easy matter. One of the pair of buffaloes had lost her calf just before being chosen to go aboard the Ark, and she told Yessah she would be only too pleased to be milked. Next, there were plenty of eggs: a lot of hen birds had already begun to lay, and Yessah was able to choose from many different sorts. As for vegetables and fruit, these were kept in Mrs Noah's store; but when her back was turned, two furry little grey

shapes popped in, and out again, with a bunch of grapes and a handful of radishes. The monkeys were quick and careful, and Mrs Noah never noticed them.

So, at last, Yessah sat down to eat a splendid breakfast, deep in the lowest, darkest part of the belly of the Ark.

He drank thirstily from a great pitcher of warm buffalo milk, and chewed hungrily on the radishes. Then he swallowed the grapes whole, pips and all.

Finally he ate a raw egg. Which may not sound much, but it was an ostrich's egg.

'Lovely!' he said, rubbing his tummy. 'Now I simply must sleep. I can't keep my eyes open.'

'Not yet, Yessah,' said the bull elephant, 'first, a bath.' He stuck his trunk out of a port-hole and sucked, then squirted a great jet of water over Yessah, again and again, till all the dirt and filth was washed away. Now Yessah stood clean but shivering in his soaking-wet clothes.

'We'll soon warm you up,' said one of the grizzly bears, and she took the little man in her arms, hugging him very carefully against her hot, hairy chest until he was as dry as a bone.

'Now you can sleep, Master,' cooed Peace and Goodwill, and Yessah saw that the most comfortable bed you can imagine had been made for him.

For a mattress, there were two great tigers, lying back to back; Yessah stretched himself between them, upon the striped velvet of their glowing hides. He rested his weary head on a pillow of warm, furry wolfskin (with a wolf inside it). Just as he was dropping off to sleep, he felt as though the lightest, softest coverlet had been pulled over him to keep him cosy, for down fluttered a blanket of little birds – finches, robins, wrens and many more, one pair of each – and they settled gently upon Noah's brother, spreading their small wings over him.

Throughout that day Yessah slept. Three times Noah sent his sons in turn, to see that all was well below decks, first Shem, then Ham, and lastly Japheth; but each had difficulty in carrying out the order.

Shem fell flat on his face on the upper deck when something that hissed wound itself round his ankles. Ham, on the middle deck, had a sharp disagreement with a porcupine. Japheth went furthest, actually beginning to climb down the ladder that led to the lowest deck, when suddenly he heard a deep, rumbling sound, and looked down to see a lion's mouth underneath him, wide open.

However, each son told his father that all was well, and Yessah slept soundly on his luxurious bed, warm and dry.

High above him, Noah stood gazing across the waste of waters while the never-ending rain ran down the slopes of his great craggy face and dripped from the cliff of his beard.

He was not thinking of his wife, or of his sons and their wives, or the animals, or the Ark itself. He was thinking about his brother.

Noah did not doubt, for he had great faith, that one day the Flood would subside and the Ark would come to rest on dry land. Then all the creatures would be let go, to breed and fill the empty land with their offspring. Noah's sons would found great families of their own to form a mighty tribe of men with Noah himself at the head of it, Mrs Noah by his side. All that was fine, and just as it should be, but what about that scrawny old brother of his? He had no wife, no children; he would be of no use in the brave new world ahead. Just an extra mouth to feed, thought Noah, and a fussy one at that. Vegetarian indeed!

'He's useful to me at present, so I'll put up with him till the end of the voyage,' growled Noah, and the thunder growled back at him. 'But once the animals are gone, he'll have to go too, for good. No need for future generations to know that the great Noah ever had a brother!'

Chapter Five

It is an interesting fact (which few people know) that the Ark was at one time in danger of sinking. If that had happened, of course, not even a few people would have known about it. No one would have known, because Noah's family would have drowned and left a world empty of human beings for evermore.

Luckily there was one man aboard the Ark who saved it from going down. It wasn't Shem, or Ham, or Japheth, or even Noah himself: it was Noah's brother.

It happened when the Ark had been afloat for three weeks. Noah had just taken out his knife and cut the twenty-first notch in the back of Mrs Noah's neck. It wasn't the real Mrs Noah, but a wooden figure-head carved to look like her and fixed to the prow of the boat. Yessah had made it when they

were building the Ark. He was brilliant at carving things like animals from wood, so Noah told him to make a likeness of his wife. Mrs Noah was not especially good-looking so Yessah was careful to make the carving flattering, giving her a fine curved nose and large eyes to gaze out over the limitless expanse of water.

However, once the Ark was afloat, no one could see the face of the figure-head. They would have been surprised at the change in it. One day early in the voyage, when Mrs Noah had been especially bossy to Yessah, shouting, 'Hey you! Do this,' and 'Hey you! Do that,' all morning, he had decided to get his own back. He waited till no one was looking, and then he climbed out on to the figure-head. With a few deft cuts he altered its appearance.

Little did Noah know, as he made the twenty-first notch, that Mrs Noah's nose was now an ugly blob and her eyes were horribly crossed. Little did he know either, that day or indeed ever, what was happening on the lowest deck.

Nobody had noticed that over those first three weeks the Ark had been gradually settling lower and lower in the water. It hadn't sprung any leaks, for the pitch had kept its hull quite watertight, and it hadn't run against any rocks, for even the tops of the mountains were far below. What had happened, quite simply, was this: twenty-one days and nights of non-stop, pouring rain had made every plank of its gopher-wood timbers soggy, soaking and waterlogged. The Ark was sinking under its own weight.

Yessah was busy on the lowest deck, and the first he knew of it was when water began dribbling over the edge of the port-holes. (There were six port-holes at this level, three to a side. A cubit is the length from a man's elbow to the end of his middle finger, and when the Ark first floated, each port-hole was 4 cubits above the water-level.) Now, as Yessah poked his head out, he found to his horror that the surface of the Flood was just under his nose. Once it began to pour in, the Ark would settle deeper and deeper till, at last, it sank like a stone.

There wasn't a moment to lose: the port-holes must be blocked. But how? There was only one way to block them, Yessah realized – with animals; but if he asked the animals to stick their heads through the holes, they would drown. Their bottoms, then. Yes! That was it! The port-holes must be blocked by bottoms – the biggest bottoms he could find!

Within minutes Yessah had the situation under control. He called up the two elephants, the two hippos, and the two rhinos, and backed them up

against the port-holes. Each animal faced its mate on the opposite side, and so the boat was kept on an even keel. Not a drop of water came in.

To relieve them, Yessah formed a team of six bears: two polar, two black and two grizzly. Their bottoms were not as big, and, when they took their turn, some water did seep in but the elephants soon pumped it out again.

And so, you see, mankind was saved by the quick thinking of one little old bald-headed man.

By the time Noah had cut his twenty-eighth notch in Mrs Noah's neck, the danger (of which he knew nothing) was mostly over. The gopher wood had soaked up all the water it could, and the Ark rode no lower. Certainly it sailed very slowly and sluggishly but that didn't matter: it wasn't going anywhere special.

So the days passed, with no sign of any change in the weather. The rain fell relentlessly upon the dark waters that covered the earth. Yessah worked hard looking after the animals, and the animals in their turn looked after him.

Every day they made sure he was well fed. The cow buffalo gave plenty of rich milk, the monkeys stole all sorts of fruit and vegetables from the store; and as for eggs, Yessah had the choice of hundreds of different kinds. Every night his lovely warm, living bed was ready for him.

Up in the galley, Mrs Noah and her daughters-in-law worked hard too, cooking great meals of meat for their men on a stove that was always in danger of going out in all that wet. Mrs Noah grew more and more crusty, shouting 'Hey you!' at Yessah whenever she caught sight of him (which he made sure was as seldom as possible).

On the upper deck, Shem, Ham and Japheth worked sulkily, looking after the small creatures that lived up there: little snakes, frogs, lizards and various beetles; they did not venture down into either of the lower decks any more and so were always soaking wet.

Wettest of all was Noah on the poop-deck, watching always for some sign of the end of the Flood.

Increasingly he longed for the moment when the Ark should settle on dry land and he could be rid of his bleating, lowing, roaring, barking, squawk-ing, smelly cargo, and especially that useless old brother of his.

On the morning he cut his fortieth notch on the figure-head, he decided to act.

'Send for my brother!' he bellowed down to Mrs Noah, and she in turn yelled down to Yessah.

'Hey you!' she hollered. 'Noah wants you!'

Hastily Noah's brother swallowed the last mouthful of a delicious omelette made from pea-cocks' and pheasants' eggs, and climbed to the poop-deck.

'Yessah?' he said.

'Fetch me a bird, Brother,' said Noah, 'I want to send one out to see if there's any sign of dry land.'

So Yessah fetched one of the ravens, which flew till it was out of sight. They waited, but it never returned.

'Fetch another,' said Noah angrily; and then a thought struck him.

'Fetch a dove,' he said.

Yessah went weak at the knees. Oh, not my dear

Peace or my dear Goodwill, he thought frantically,
I couldn't bear to lose one of them.

'A turtle-dove, Noah?' he said in a pleading
voice. 'Or a rock-dove?'

'No,' said Noah. 'One of your precious white
ones.'

Chapter Six

Down in the lowest, darkest part of the belly of the Ark, the elephants had just finished their first task of the day, pumping water out, when Yessah climbed down the ladder. Even in the semi-darkness they could see his face was white, as white as his two friends who came fluttering to perch on his thin shoulders.

'Why, whatever is the matter, best of men?' trumpeted the cow elephant, and at the sound of her voice the other beasts gathered round. Only the hen raven sat black and silent upon her perch.

'What is it, Master?' asked Peace and Goodwill.

'The raven,' said Yessah slowly. 'He has not returned. Now Noah wants one of you, my dears, to fly out and look for land.'

'Ah!' breathed the listening crowd, for they knew how much the doves meant to Noah's brother.

'What Noah wants is one thing,' said Peace.

45

'But what you want is another,' said Goodwill.

'Do *you* want one of us to go, Master?' they said.

Yessah hesitated.

'Oh dear!' he cried miserably. 'I could not *order* either of you to undertake so dangerous a task. Even if you found the dry land for which we all long, you might never find your way back to the Ark again. I might never see you again.'

'Nevermore!' croaked the hen raven.

For a moment all the animals were silent, and then 'Rubbish!' said Peace in a cheery voice. 'Of course you will see me again, Master.'

'Wait! Why you? Let me go!' cried Goodwill to his mate, but, before he could make a move, she flew out of the nearest port-hole.

Yessah spent the rest of the day in an agony of suspense. He could not keep his mind on his work for worrying about Peace; he fed hay to the lions and tigers, and gave the giraffes a huge bone each, much to their surprise.

In the afternoon he was summoned to the

poop-deck, where he found Noah with a very tired-looking white dove upon his wrist. Yessah took Peace below, and dried and warmed her, then Goodwill brought food to his mate and popped it into her gaping beak as though she were a nestling chick.

'Nothing,' she said, when at last she was rested. 'There was nothing but water and yet more water. The world is one enormous sea.'

Yessah spent the next few days worrying that Peace might be sent out again, and just when he had begun to relax a little and forget about it, she was.

There were forty-seven notches on the neck of the figure-head when, at Noah's orders, Peace flew away once more.

'Try not to worry, my dear,' said Yessah to Goodwill, smoothing his feathers. 'She'll come back, I'm sure,' and she did, just before sundown. But this time she carried something in her beak.

Everyone came running at Noah's great shout.

'Behold!' he cried to the family.

And they beheld.

'It's a dove,' said Ham, who wasn't very bright.

Japheth and Shem were not much better.

'It's got something in its beak,' said one.

'Looks like a twig with leaves on it,' said the other.

Mrs Noah was the best of a bad bunch. She was after all a cook, and cooks used oil, and oil came from olives.

'It's an olive twig,' she said.

'Of course it's an olive twig!' roared Noah. 'Any fool can see that. But where did it come from?'

'Off an olive tree?' said Ham hopefully.

'Well, what does that mean, you dolt?' shouted Noah. 'Can none of you see what it means?'

His brick-red face turned purple.

'Begone!' he bellowed at the family.

And they bewent.

Only Yessah stood his ground, though he was shaking with fear at his brother's anger.

'Well?' shouted Noah.

'It m-means that the Flood is beginning to go down. Somewhere, there is a tree sticking up above the water.'

'You're not as stupid as you look,' said Noah.

'P-please,' said Yessah, 'can I have my dove back?'

'Take your bird,' growled Noah, 'but I shall want it again, one week from today.'

There was great excitement as news of the olive twig spread round the boat, the boat in which they had all been confined for so long, cramped, damp,

and often sea-sick. All the animals were indeed heartily sick of the sea and longing to stretch their legs, or their wings, or their coils once again.

'How we will run!' cried the gazelles.

'How we will soar!' cried the eagles.

'How we will hop!' cried the kangaroos.

'How we will climb!' cried the monkeys.

'How we will eat ants!' cried the anteaters.

The ants just cried.

Seven more days passed; Noah cut the fifty-fourth
notch in the back of Mrs Noah's neck, and away
went Peace for the third time.

Noah's brother watched until she disappeared
from sight. He held Goodwill gently in his hands.

'Don't worry, my dear,' he said once again. 'She
will come back.'

They watched and they waited, they waited and they watched, that day and for many days, for the dove called Peace to return to the Ark. But she did not return.

Chapter Seven

Yessah was very unhappy at the loss of Peace, and it did not help to hear the sad voice of Goodwill mourning softly for his mate. But then one day something happened that shook both of them out of their misery. In fact it shook everyone aboard. Suddenly, with a crash, the Ark ran aground!

At the impact, Yessah thought they had hit a whale. He rushed to the nearest port-hole and saw, to his amazement, a wall of rock. It was the same on the other side of the boat. He ran up on to the upper deck.

The boat was held firmly in the trough of a V-shaped outcrop, on the top of what seemed to be a small island. But as the family watched, they saw the water level receding like an outgoing tide. The Ark was in fact stuck, high and dry, on top of a mountain.

There did not appear to be much damage, except to the figure-head; Mrs Noah's face, Yessah was not sorry to see, had taken a bashing. They all turned to look at Noah standing up above them on the poop-deck.

'Where are we, Father?' shouted Shem.

Noah stood tall, feet firmly planted on the deck that would never move beneath him again. He threw wide his arms and raised his great bearded face to the heavens, and, after a quick peep down to make sure they were all watching, cried in ringing tones, 'Oh, people of Noah! We are upon a mountain!'

'What's it called, Father?' shouted Japheth.

Noah hesitated. He hadn't a clue, but it would never do for the all-knowing Noah to admit this. Then he had a piece of luck: when the boat had struck the rock, the two rats on board had reacted as rats always do.

'It's a sinking ship!' cried one.

'Then we'll leave it!' cried the other.

Now they ran across the upper deck on their

way to leap over the side in such haste that one of them scuttled across Mrs Noah's feet, just after Japheth had asked his question.

'It . . . is . . . called . . .' began Noah slowly and, at that instant, Mrs Noah yelled, 'Ar! A rat!'

Ham grinned his rather foolish grin.

'Father!' he shouted. 'Mother says it's called Ararat.'

'She took the word right out of my mouth,' said Noah. 'We are indeed, as I was about to tell you, upon the summit of Mount Ararat. Let down the gangway!'

And Shem, Ham and Japheth let it down.

It is an interesting fact (which few people know) that Noah did not allow all the animals to go after the Flood. Oh no. He was not so silly. He knew that farming would be the only life for his family, and that their first task was to begin the breeding of flocks and herds to feed the great tribe, as yet unborn, of which he would be the head.

So he ordered his sons to keep back the buffaloes, the sheep and the goats; and animals to provide stock for riding upon, or for pulling ploughs and carts, like the donkeys and the camels; and many other kinds of beasts and birds that a farmer would need. By nightfall, these were the only creatures left in the Ark. The rest were gone. The birds had flown, except for two, one white and one black, that had no mate; the animals had marched (and hopped, and crawled, and wriggled), two by two down the gangway, down the mountainside, away into the drying world.

The next morning Noah called a family conference on the poop-deck, but first he needed Yessah out of the way. He sent for his brother.

'Brother,' he said, 'go down to the bottom of Mount Ararat and have a good look at the lie of the land. Go to the west, then come back and tell me. No hurry.'

'Yessah,' said Noah's brother.

Noah watched the thin, bald-headed figure

picking his way down the slopes, and then turned to the others.

'My brother,' he said, 'has gone west. He will not be back for some while.'

Mrs Noah sniffed. 'Pity he has to come back at all,' she said, 'he's only going to be a burden to us when we set out.'

Noah looked at the others.

'Is that the feeling of you all?' he said.

Shem, Ham, Japheth and their wives nodded their heads vigorously.

'We don't want him tagging along with us, Father,' said Shem.

'Just another mouth to feed,' said Japheth.

'On cabbages,' said Ham, grinning, 'like an old rabbit.'

'You are speaking,' said Noah severely, 'of Hazardikladoram, brother of Noah.'

'No one need ever know, Noah,' said Mrs Noah. 'When they come to tell the history of the great Noah, no one need ever know that he had a brother.'

'How then shall we be rid of him?' said Noah. He suspected that Ham or his brothers would cheerfully have wrung the old rabbit's neck, but he did not want to be the one to suggest it.

'Easy,' said Mrs Noah. 'He can have this filthy old Ark to himself. He's a vegetarian; he can finish up the hay. Let us take the rest of the animals and go; he's gone west, we'll go east. Now – fast!'

She took a sly look at her husband.

'If Noah so decrees,' she added.

Noah gave a fine imitation of a man forced, much against his will, to leave his only brother. He stared sadly westward, smote himself upon the brow and let out a long shuddering sigh.

'I so decree,' he said at last in a hollow voice, and off the others hurried to get things ready.

Noah climbed down from the poop-deck and walked forward to the prow of the boat to the disfigured figure-head. He patted the top of Mrs Noah's gopher-wood head.

'You took the words right out of my mouth,' he said. 'One day, men will write in a great book about the beginnings of the world. Noah's name will be written large, and the story of Noah's Ark; and the names of Noah's sons and their sons and

their sons' sons that shall found all the nations of
the earth. But nowhere in its pages will you find
the name of Hazardikladoram.'

He was right. You won't.

Chapter Eight

When Yessah reached the bottom of the mountain, he found everything looking pretty strange. The Flood had gone down miraculously, but still there were great pools and lakes everywhere. The trees appeared limp and soggy, like giant seaweeds, from being under water for such a time.

But already the world looked so much better. The golden sun was shining again, the sky was blue. As Yessah looked up into it he saw, high above, a large black bird gliding and wheeling as though it were searching for something below. When it saw Yessah, it shut its wings and dived towards him. It was the male raven that Noah had sent out on the fortieth day.

'Am I glad to see you!' croaked the bird, as it landed and hopped up to Noah's brother. 'I searched the world for that beastly boat and couldn't find it. I've been away ages. My mate will

be raven mad. Where is she?'

Yessah pointed to the summit.

'Before you go,' he said, 'tell me. Have you seen any sign of my white dove, Peace?'

'Afraid not,' said the raven. 'I only saw seabirds and waterfowl. Sorry!' And he flapped away up the western slopes of Mount Ararat.

Yessah explored the plain at the mountain's foot for some time, and then he set off to return to the Ark.

It was long past midday when at last he neared it, though the stable smell of it came to him on the wind some while before. Smell and noise, thought Yessah, that's what I shall always remember about the voyage, especially noise. Twenty-four-hour noise it was: first from the creatures of the day and then from those of the night, and from Noah bawling orders and Mrs Noah yelling 'Hey you!' Funny, it seems strangely quiet now.

Yessah climbed the gangway and went aft to the poop-deck.

'Noah!' he called, but there was no reply.

He searched the upper deck. There was no sign of his three nephews, and no animals.

On the middle deck, the galley was empty, the stove cold, and again all the beasts were gone. He looked in Mrs Noah's store to see what was left, but there was only one wrinkled apple.

It was the same on his own deck, the bottom deck – the lowest, darkest part of the belly of the Ark. There was not a single creature to be seen. Where's Goodwill, thought Yessah, surely he has not left me?

Once again he searched the boat calling, 'Goodwill! Goodwill! Where are you, my dear? Come to old Yessah,' but there was no answer.

There was no sound to be heard but the sigh of the wind as Noah's brother sat eating a mouldy apple in an empty boat on top of a lonely mountain.

Just for a moment Yessah felt very sorry for himself, but he was a tough old man, and he had had 708 years to learn one of life's most useful lessons. Whenever you feel really depressed, count your blessings. Yessah counted his.

First, he was alive, which he would not have been if his brother had not ordered the building of the Ark, nor indeed if the python had not rescued him at the start of the Flood, or if the other animals had not nursed and tended him.

Which led him to count his second blessing, the company of the animals. He would never be lonely wherever he went, even though now he had no family.

This led him to count his third blessing, that now he had no family.

At that moment he knew for certain that he wasn't going to miss any of them for one second, ever again. There were only two living things in the world that he was missing, terribly. He could only hope that Goodwill might find his mate, Peace, once more.

Thinking about the doves made Yessah look up into the heavens and he noticed what a beautiful evening it was, warm and sunny. And, as he looked, he saw to his amazement a great arch of colour beginning to form in the sky.

Far away to the east, where a little last rain was still falling, Noah and his party saw it too as they drove their beasts onward. It curved down from

the heavens and seemed to plunge into the ground just ahead of them. They pressed on, hoping to reach the end of it, yet it always eluded them.

But the western end of the great, glowing arch fell full upon Yessah, as he sat in the empty Ark and marvelled. He had never seen such a thing before. There had never been such a thing before.

Seven brilliant colours shone down upon him – red, orange, yellow, green, blue, indigo and violet – and then suddenly an eighth was added, as two snow-white shapes came winging down the curve of the rainbow and settled upon the thin shoulders of Noah's brother. 'Peace,' said one softly in his left ear, and 'Goodwill,' said the other in his right.

It is an interesting fact (which everybody knows) that the children of Noah fathered all the nations of the earth; nations that to this day quarrel with each other, fight with each other, torture and starve and kill each other, with a greed and cruelty that not one of the animals in the Ark would possibly have understood.

Everybody knows that.

But do you know what happened to Noah's brother? I'll tell you.

With Peace and Goodwill, he lived happily. Ever after.

More Books from Puffin

COME BACK SOON

Judy Gardiner

Val's family seem quite an odd bunch and their life is hectic but happy. But then Val's mother walks out on them and Val's carefree life is suddenly quite different. This is a moving but funny story.

AMY' EYES

Richard Kennedy

When a doll changes into a man it means that anything might happen . . . and in this magical story all kinds of strange and wonderful things do happen to Amy and her sailor doll, the Captain. Together they set off on a fantastic journey on a quest for treasure more valuable than mere gold.

ASTERCOTE

Penelope Lively

Astercote village was destroyed by plague in the fourteenth century and Mair and her brother Peter find themselves caught up in a strange adventure when an ancient superstition is resurrected.

THE HOUNDS OF THE MÓRRÍGAN

Pat O'Shea

When the Great Queen Mórrígan, evil creature from the world of Irish mythology, returns to destroy the world, Pidge and Brigit are the children chosen to thwart her. How they go about it makes an hilarious, moving story, full of totally original and unforgettable characters.

THE PRIME MINISTER'S BRAIN
Gillian Cross

The fiendish DEMON HEADMASTER plans to gain control of No. 10 Downing Street and lure the Prime Minister into his evil clutches.

JASON BODGER AND THE PRIORY GHOST
Gene Kemp

A ghost story, both funny and exciting, about Jason, the bane of every teacher's life, who is pursued by the ghost of a little nun from the twelfth century!

HALFWAY ACROSS THE GALAXY AND TURN LEFT
Robin Klein

A humorous account of what happens to a family banished from their planet Zygron, when they have to spend a period of exile on Earth.

SUPER GRAN TO THE RESCUE
Forrest Wilson

The punchpacking, baddiebiffing escapades of the worlds' No. 1 senior citizen superhero – Super Gran! Now a devastating series on ITV!

TOM TIDDLER'S GROUND
John Rowe Townsend

Vic and Brain are given an old rowing boat which leads to the unravelling of a mystery and a happy reunion of two friends. An exciting adventure story.

WOOF!

Allan Ahlberg

Eric is a perfectly ordinary boy. Perfectly ordinary, that is, until the night when, safely tucked up in bed, he slowly turns into a dog! Fritz Wegner's drawings superbly illustrate this funny and exciting story.

VERA PRATT AND THE FALSE MOUSTACHES

Brough Girling

There were times when Wally Pratt wished his mum was more ordinary and not the fanatic mechanic she was, but when he and his friends find themselves caught up in a real 'cops and robbers' affair, he is more than glad to have his mum, Vera, to help them.

SADDLEBOTTOM

Dick King Smith

Hilarious adventures of a Wessex Saddleback pig whose white saddle is in the wrong place, to the chagrin of his mother.

SLADE

John Tully

Slade has a mission – to investigate life on Earth. When Eddie discovers the truth about Slade he gets a whole lot more adventure than he bargained for.

A TASTE OF BLACKBERRIES

Doris Buchanan Smith

The moving story about a young boy who has to come to terms with the tragic death of his best friend and the guilty feeling that he could somehow have saved him.

JELLYBEAN

Tessa Duder

A sensitive modern novel about Geraldine, alias 'Jellybean', who leads a rather solitary life as the only child of a single parent. She's tired of having to fit in with her mother's busy schedule, but a new friend and a performance of 'The Nutcracker Suite' change everything.

THE PRIESTS OF FERRIS

Maurice Gee

Susan Ferris and her cousin Nick return to the world of O which they had saved from the evil Halfmen, only to find that O is now ruled by cruel and ruthless priests. Can they save the inhabitants of O from tyranny? An action-packed and gripping story by the author of prize-winning *The Halfmen of O*.

THE SEA IS SINGING

Rosalind Kerven

In her seaside Shetland home, Tess is torn between the plight of the whales and loyalty to her father and his job on the oil rig. A haunting and thought-provoking novel.

BACK HOME

Michelle Magorian

A marvellously gripping story of an irrepressible girl's struggle to adjust to a new life. Twelve-year-old Rusty, who had been evacuated to the United States when she was seven, returns to the grey austerity of post-war Britain.

THE BEAST MASTER

André Norton

Spine-chilling science fiction – treachery and revenge! Hosteen Storm is a man with a mission to find and punish Brad Quade, the man who killed his father long ago on Terra, the planet where life no longer exists.